# Poetic Verses

# Poetic Verses

*Gamaliel H. Gooding*

iUniverse, Inc.

New York   Bloomington

iUniverse books may be ordered through booksellers or by contacting:

iUniverse
1663 Liberty Drive
Bloomington, IN 47403
www.iuniverse.com
1-800-Authors (1-800-288-4677)

ISBN: 978-1-4401-7830-6 (sc)
ISBN: 978-1-4401-7831-3 (ebook)

Printed in the United States of America

iUniverse rev. date: 11/04/2009

# CONTENTS

# POETIC VERSES

# THIS BOOK OF POETRY IS
# DEDICATED TO
# MY WIFE
# ELIVRA GOODING

# INTRODUCTION

*I have attempted to share life's experiences, good, bad and indifferent in a way that is clear and tasteful to the reader. Mostly, all of my work deals with reality, my personal concept of how things are, the way I think things should be, and ultimately, the way I think things should turn out.*

*I am fortunate enough to have had parents that were not only Christians, but Ministers. Because of my religious background and upbringing, my insights are critical when engaged in relations of husband and wife, family, friends and associates.*

*I hope when you read my work, you will enjoy it as much as I did creating it. Maybe in some small way, you maybe inspired to reach out to someone, if you haven't already. My philosophy is there is no better medicine for the soul then caring.*

*The Author*

# ACKNOWLEDGEMENTS

*I would like to thank my wife, Elvira and my son Hasani, for their support.*

*They were always there to cheer me on whenever my thoughts became evasive. I am thankful for the support of my brothers, Curtis and Donald, and all of my In-Laws. I am very grateful for all the support I received from my co-workers at the Dorchester House. I am thankful for the support and encouragement of Ms. Carolyn Bernier, who was not only my boss, but one of my very best friends. Thanks so much to Bob who also lived at the Dorchester House at the time this book was being written. I know Bob can't wait to read his poem (My Bob). A special thanks to Anna, who can't wait to read the poem that was written about her daughter Malissa. Thanks to Sherly for inspiring me to write, (Should I Believe My Eyes). Thanks to Mbaye who inspired me to write the (Road Less Traveled).*

*It would be remissed of me if I did not give thanks to him who created me (God), and made all of this possible.*

*The Author: Gamaliel H. Gooding*

# ELVIRA'S STAR

*A Special Dedication to Mother*

*I strongly feel that any writing skills that I may have, I owe to my Mother, the late Reverend Carrie A. Gooding, Devout Evangelist and Spiritual Healer. She provided a base for learning before school age, by spending countless hours teaching me my (ABC) how to spell and form sentences. All of this transpired before I was five years of age. She insisted that being able to speak clearly and correctly were the keys to providing for your listening and reading audience a vivid picture of your thoughts.*

*She instilled in me from a very early age the importance of verbal and written communication. In All of my writings, I have attempted to apply what she taught me.*

*I hope in some small way, I have done her justice.*

# A Wild Flower

*How unfair they are with*
*their array of colors, majestic*
*display of beauty and*
*dignity in which they lay clean.*

*On the hillsides, mountain tops,*
*highways, byways, and along*
*side the river's edge,*
*they cannot be contained.*

*Under all manner of conditions,*
*they flourish when others perish.*
*Their strength is hidden by their frailty,*
*but destined to beautify the earth.*

*For you are like a wild flower, so*
*slender and curvaceous so titillating to*
*the senses, with the quickness of mind*
*and a body for sin.*

*I long to touch the perfectly created*
*petals and caress the elongated stems,*
*But I awake to find no end,*
*Only to begin again.*

# America at War

*On September 11, 2001, tyranny raised its head.*
*This day shall forever be imprinted in our*
*minds and hearts.*

*You can rest assured that those who died*
*and those who were injured, can rest in the comfort*
*of knowing that their sacrifice was not in vain.*

*From this act of tyranny, shall rise out*
*of the ashes of death and destruction, a love*
*and unity in measures unprecedented.*

*The avenging Angels shall stretch out their*
*arms of protection and their hands will*
*be bearing swords of fire and brimstone.*

*The enemy's punishment shall be rendered with*
*a precision never witness. It shall be with*
*an exactness and a finality.*

*And once again, this great country shall*
*prevail, and the light of freedom shall once*
*again shine.*

# Clara Hood

*That old building with shattered windows*
*and doors of splintered wood,*
*vacant rooms with ghostly sounds*
*and the foot prints of Clara Hood.*

*With her weathered skin*
*and piercing eyes,*
*her form had begin to*
*materialize.*

*Her fainting voice and*
*slender frame,*
*her knife like finger nails*
*and her hickory walking cane.*

*Like yesterday, I can remember*
*the floor stained with blood,*
*the ax resting on the old wooden stove,*
*dismembered on the floor was Mr. Hood.*

# Elvira, You are Crystal

*Crystal is the personification of*
*purity, strength and light.*
*It is multifaceted in its infusions*
*that exemplifies your life in*
*different stages.*

*It is flawless in its mirrored image,*
*which exemplifies the perfection*
*of God's creation and his infinite wisdom*
*involved in his thought process.*

*The strength of crystal is a*
*reflection of the binding process of you*
*It gives you the will to excel,*
*even in times of trials and tribulations.*

*The unique artistry involved in the*
*creation of crystal is a reflection of*
*your inner and outer beauty, which I*
*See is a reflection of you.*

*The fire that emanates from crystal*
*reflects your zest for life and*
*your endless desire*
*to reach out to others.*

# *Faith*

*In the dark we walk with*
*that dreadful fear of sinking.*

*In silence we stand with*
*that dreadful fear of thinking.*

*In life we think of death, in*
*doing so we are deceived.*

*What heights of glory are in our sight?*
*what wonders we could achieve.*

*Desirous we re of odious things,*
*the beast of the dark control us.*

*Like children, we dream of life like toys*
*that which gives us pleasure we trust.*

*If only we would begin the journey*
*with one step of confidence.*

*Enjoying the experience and freedom*
*given with our creator's consent.*

# Father

*Traveling far,*
*energy low,*
*light changed to darkness*
*many miles ago.*

*Trying to reach home*
*before his end.*
*Traveling this road alone*
*all over again*

*Last chance café*
*is up ahead.*
*I will pull in, not to stay,*
*just for coffee and short bread.*

*Then it came to me,*
*his heart is weak*
*this is my father I got to see,*
*maybe the last chance we have to speak.*

*For a lesson learned*
*is wisdom gained?*
*Never to be late again*
*for this I yearned,*

*just to whisper his name,*

*Father.*

# Grandmother

*It was not so long ago*
*that you nurtured me, walked*
*with me and held my hand.*

*I was little then.*

*You walked and talked with me*
*and told me biblical stories of*
*creation and how it all begin.*

*As I grew older you would*
*still walk and talk with me about*
*dreams of a larger plan.*

*I was getting older then.*

*And then! Your teaching increased, you*
*became more aggressive, you were molding me*
*into what you thought I should be as a man.*

*I am grateful for having a Grandmother*
*who was patient with me and*
*kept me safe.*

*I am older now.*

*I now understand why you walked*
*with me and had those talks under*
*that old Oak tree.*

*Now that God in his infinite wisdom*
*has called you home, I know*
*your work is done.*

*I cherish those precious times*
*God allowed you to spend*
*with your Grandson.*

# To My Wife on Her Birthday

*I find you so special in every way,*
*I learned something special and*
*exciting about you each passing day.*

*I have watched you overcome pain and*
*sadness, I have witnessed your tears.  I have*
*watch you grow during these thirty-two years.*

*I have tried to be strong for you in*
*my weakest hour.*
*I have tried to nurture you as a*
*gardener would his flowers.*

*I have always seen in you a pure heart*
*and the uncanny ability to carry on the fight.*
*Even when things seemed wrong.*
*They always turned out right.*

*I have always admired the greatness of*
*your stature and the strength of*
*your convictions.  How you rely on past*
*experiences and your intuition.*

*Your Birthday is very special to me*
*because I have you in my life.  It*
*is even more special to me*
*because you are my wife*

*Happy Birthday*

## *Elvira*
## *Having You as My Wife*

*I find you witty,*
*Intelligent, full of fire and energy.*

*Wonderful, ingenious,*
*funny, endearing*
*and innovating.*

*Dedicated to your*
*aspirations and my*
*happiness.*

*Loves to share with your*
*family and friends and*
*those who are less fortunate.*

*Strong and unyielding*
*in your views and*
*convictions.*

*I find you to be a*
*loving, caring and*
*giving person.*

*I could have made no better choice in*
*Choosing you for my*
*Life long partner*
*in Holy Matrimony.*

*From this day forward*
*I promise to always love, cherish*
*and protect you.*

# He Who Created You

He who created you and gave your free will,
gave you a pathway to peace and joy.
With joy come struggling in the fields,
moving obstacles that the devil deployed.

Take heed not to grovel at the feet of success,
created by your earthly efforts and creative mind.
Be wise and prudent as you prepare for this test,
for the journey of life can be very unkind.

Beware of those who covet you under pretense.
What is your true love worth to yourself and others?
Never leave unguarded the gate of consent,
for it is as precious as a father and mother.

As you take this walk thru life,
undaunted, full of vigor and pride.
Nothing is important and nothing will suffice,
other then using your creative will to survive.

You must always remember he who created you,
gave you free will, peace and joy.
Do not be duped by words of no substance,
beware of grown men's gifts and little boys toys.

# I Am

*I think, therefore I am.*
*I am, therefore I exist.*
*I exist, therefore, I have purpose.*
*I have purpose, therefore I must function.*

*I must function, therefore, I must*
*seek clarity of my purpose for existing.*
*I grow in increments, therefore I must retain.*
*that which I retain, I must endeavor to understand.*

*With wisdom and clarity of purpose,*
*I will begin my journeys.*
*I pray that at the end of my journey,*
*my destiny will have manifested itself.*

*Only then can I say with some degree of*
*absolution, my existence has not been in vain.*
*In my world of mediocrity I will have created*
*some small space of harmony from discord.*

*From diversity, an array of mixed blessings*
*will have been planted for a future generation.*

# Malissa

*A perfect face rapped in Nordic*
*hair that glitters in the sunlight.*

*Eyes that twinkles, a smile that*
*radiates warmth and passion.*

*A laugh that brightens' one's day.*
*Her voice can soothe the savage beast.*

*Her skin is milky white with a cloud*
*like softness, her body is a measure*

*Of perfect numbers.  She  can be*
*childlike in her actions, she can*

*Exude sensuality that is boundless*
*in energy.  Her presence will*

*Lift your spirit*

*She is Malissa*

# Mbaye Ndour

*Roads with smooth pathways, I
refused to trod.
I will focus my energy on roads
less traveled.*

*Roads that I might learn the
true path and be enlightened
by it's challenges and teachings.*

*I discovered early in life,
from one corner of the world
to the other,*

*All men desires the same
knowledge that they might
Acquire skills.*

*Love that they might share
and a spiritual enlightenment
that they might have peace.*

*This is Mbaye Ndour's dream*

## Africa
## From A Mountain to a Molehill

Families are starving,
children are dying
from senseless wars.

By their own people
they are denied their homes
to return no more.

Dried up fields
waterless wells
with no seeds to sow.

After miles of traveling
over rugged terrain
with no place to go.

Humanity surges forward over
shadowed by the cruelty of man.
Humanity cry for help falls on deaf ears.

But the end is near,
that which is a mountain
will be reduced to a molehill.

That which was a molehill
shall consume the mountain
and reign forever with love.

From the earth will come forth salt
and flavor shall return to the land,
valleys will run red with the enemy's blood.

Peace will forever be restored.

# Mother

*Before my earthly conception,*
*I was bless by the creator*
*who knew me in him.*

*With my earthly birth,*
*I was bless again with an earthly*
*mother who knew and served him.*

*As a child I would acknowledge*
*her kindness with an angelic smile,*
*and touch the tip of her nose.*

*We were of one mind, body and spirit.*
*my mother knew my every need. I don't*
*remember shedding tears for any length of time.*

*The days when food was scarce, no*
*milk bread or meat was near,*
*she didn't worry, she knew her father.*

*She only had to go behind close doors,*
*and talk to him. He always*
*answered whenever she call on him.*

*Now that she is gone from the earthly realm,*
*I don't have to fear. She doesn't have*
*to pray from a distance.*

*Now she is sitting beside him.*
*She can talk to him face to face about*
*my needs, and they are still being met.*

*She continues to be Mother*

# My Bob

*Tall and stately he stood,*
*in the shadows of the night*
*as a New York skyline*

*His walk was rhythmic*
*and purposeful,*
*his smile was divine*

*As he passed swiftly by,*
*out of the corner of my eye,*
*I caught him at a glance.*

*I found myself over shadowed*
*by his commanding presence*
*and my heart was so entranced.*

*All of these years I have*
*searched for the man of my dreams*
*one that my heart could embrace.*

*I found him in an isolated part*
*of a grand old building*
*in the doorway of a market place.*

*Now that my search is over*
*and I am free to unpack my bags,*
*I think I'll leave the bags on the ship.*

*Why take a chance carrying the bags*
*Of your past, that is full of*
*broken relationships*

*Thanks for coming into my life.*

# My dream

There is a glorious display of light
that emanates from her sparkling eyes.
Her enchanting smile engages the
senses, leaving one with no defense.

Her walk is like the movement
of the lilies swayed by the breeze
in a distant field. Her movement is
erotic and melodic in motion,
playing to a distant melody.

As she drew nearer, the smell
of her perfume was intoxicating,
almost causing a state of
hysteria.

Her skin has a silky finish,
the color of dark bronze, with a
cloud like softness. The silk garment
with its array of colors could not
hide her body of perfect curves.

The memory of her will always
be deeply imbedded in my memory.
I live only to catch a glimpse of her
once again out of the corner of my eye.

# My Valentine

*How often I have neglected to give*
*thanks for your unconditional love,*
*true dedication and your respect.*
*How often I have neglected*
*to thank you for being a*
*dedicated wife and mother.*

*For you have been my friend, my lover,*
*the backbone of my existence*
*for all these years.*
*Roses, candy, decorated cakes,*
*flamboyant parties,*
*gifts of diamonds and rubies,*
*traveling to an isolated*
*Island with beautiful flowers*
*and perfume.*

*This would seem like the perfect*
*gift to give someone as special as you.*
*but I know you so well, you would*
*prefer to continue seeing the*
*gleam in my eyes every time I come*
*home from work.*

*You would prefer the soft touches and*
*agreeable glances that we give each*
*other as we sit at the table having*
*breakfast and snacks.*

*You would prefer that we continue*
*to see in each other all*
*that's required to sustain*
*this blessed union.*

*Knowing all of this, you are still*
*deserving of all the gifts.*

*For you are a very special Valentine,*
*You are mine.*

# Mysteries

*I have looked in the mirror*
*of my soul, for an answer*
*to this mystery, with the*
*purity of a child's heart.*

*How our minds melt and*
*our feelings runs free. And*
*yet the bond of passion maintains*
*its hold in pieces and in parts.*

*This mystery of feelings and*
*illusions of grandeur that surfaces*
*so freely and uninhibited, transports*
*my entire being to a distant place.*

*In your presence, I see the best*
*of me and all that I desire right before*
*my eyes. And yet I sometimes feel like*
*an angel that has fallen from grace.*

*I long for the gentle touch of your hands,*
*the softness of your lips, the soothing*
*and melodic sound of your voice,*
*The sincerity of your feelings.*

*I have paced the floors of my*
*conscience, with all the years of my wisdom.*
*I have engaged in dialogue with the super*
*natural, but nothing is revealing.*

*It must forever remain a mystery*

# OH, How dare We Grumble

*Oh! How dare we grumble*
*at crumbs of bread,*
*when once we had our*
*choice of meat.*

*Our wines made sweet*
*with earthly flavors,*
*and patience that only*
*nature could provide.*

*But now in misery we*
*hang our heads,*
*because all our riches*
*are not deplete.*

*With self inflicted vanity*
*we destroyed our labor,*
*that which was once driven*
*Now have no drive.*

*For we should be content*
*to starve of nourishment,*
*when our bodies and minds*
*were eagle to plow the earth.*

*We failed to put in storage, the*
*bounty of that which nature*
*gave birth.*

*Oh, how dare we grumble*

# Our Angels

They listen when we pray
they guide us on our way.

The thistles and thorns of life
they move.

The pain and agony of our
mistakes, they soothe.

With love and endless mercy,
they allow us to continue the

Task of soul restoration,
that we may, during our journey

Understand the reason for our creation.

In our darkest hour they are near.

When mistakes are made
and lessons learned, they cheer.

# Patience

*My journey I am told, should be a search*
*for enlightenment of the soul. Wisdom is*
*obtained by patience so the story goes.*

*A wise man once said I must remove*
*from the center of a hill*
*one grain of sand.*

*I removed from the hill one grain of sand,*
*as the wise man said. I then asked*
*the question, why one grain?*

*He answered, if you have searched*
*and found the center,*
*it is patience you have gained.*

# Search

*I have traveled the world over,*
*relentlessly looking for someone*
*to fill this void of loneliness.*

*But I am confronted continuously*
*with the inevitable question.*
*What do you have to give*
*to that which I seek?*

# Self-centered and Vain

*This journey on this endless road*
*of discovery with it's pain and pleasure*
*light and darkness is it's main*
*color scheme.*

*But I wear suits that glitter in any kind*
*of weather, in sunshine and rain. I adorn*
*myself with accessories,*
*gold necklaces and diamond rings.*

*When I look in the mirror I see*
*the reflection of who I am not, and*
*my true self frowns at what*
*I have become, self-centered and vain.*

# Should I Believe My Eyes??

The radiant glow of your smile,
the sincerity of your piercing eyes,
the perfect contour of your lips.

The artistic rendering of a perfect body,
matched only by our grace and dignity.
The reality of being real escapes me,
but there you are, standing before me.

Should I Believe My Eyes?

Your presence lights up my day,
soothes my bewildered mind.
Your smile is like a candle in the dark
that lights my way.

Should I Believe My Eyes?

Your angelic face and expressions
places me in a peaceful place.
The reality of you being real still escapes me.

I am still wondering,

Should I Believe My Eyes?

# Soul

*Where is it?  Within us,*
*outside of us.  What is soul?*

*I believe it is the driving force*
*behind humanity.*

*That is my philosophy.  As powerful*
*as we are, with our thinking*

*and creative abilities, supposedly*
*incorporated into one organ, the brain.*

*Our bodies appear to be self-contained,*
*with self imposed restraints,*

*Self induced euphoria, impending madness,*
*on the brink of a grand display.*

*What is the driving force behind this brain?*
*Let's hope it is an educated soul.*

*Let's hope this soul has learned to rely on*
*the true treasurers of the heart.*

*Love, inner peace, and happiness.*
*Let's hope this soul is truly*

*Not blind when it comes to*
*administering justice to all.*

# The Many and The Few

*Dreary days and*
*endless nights, tormented*
*by man made dreams*
*and endless schemes.*

*Smoky clubs on*
*sunset boulevard, needle*
*infested alleyways,*
*and little girls that pimps craves*

*I long to rid myself of this self*
*imposed prison of degradation*
*of suffering and needless pain.*
*if there is no effort there is no gain.*

*I have discovered that my*
*many friends are few.*
*The many used me to no end.*
*The few helped me to begin again.*

# The Forrest Giants

*Walking down this path*
*of flowers in bloom,*
*with its dominant foliage, and*
*towering Oaks of hidden wisdom.*

*I stand in awe of these forest giants*
*that provides shade for the forest floor*
*the same giants that stood quietly*
*as the Indians prepared for war.*

*And then there is the*
*giant of all trees, the*
*Sequoias. How majestic*
*and demanding of respect.*

*They have lived through the*
*Wars of our fore-fathers,*
*They have seen the rebirth of nations,*
*after death and destruction.*

*They have witness the burden of souls*
*caused by captivity, and the bells of*
*joy when the chain were removed*
*from their weaken limbs.*

*They provided shelter and protection*
*for the inhabitants of the forest*
*Kingdom, and yet man reaches*
*out to destroy them.*

*They are eager to replace one of natures*
*greatest wonders with a wonder*
*of their own.*

*Greed!*

# The Heart That Mends

*Moments are fleeting in passion,*
*that which we hold so dear,*
*reaching aimlessly for carnal knowledge,*
*nothing we physically touch seems real.*

*Desirous we of odious things,*
*the beast of the dark controls us,*
*like children, we dream of life like toys,*
*that which gives pleasure we trust.*

*Though we give not to our existence,*
*our true purpose of being. So*
*vigorously we pursue the wishes of the beast,*
*so elusive is the heart that mends.*

*The stark reality of your inner most dreams,*
*brings to life your fear, you have*
*traveled so far, your energy is low,*
*your mind is foggy, nothing is clear.*

*Stand before the mirror of true reflection*
*and face the beast within.*
*See clarity of purpose for self, for*
*elusive no more, is the heart that mends.*

# The Path Of Self Destruction

*Walking thru the wilderness*
*of felled trees and withered flowers,*
*void of the scented fragrances,*
*replaced with burnt ambers.*

*Scorched earth where green*
*grass once flourished.*
*The sad songs of the sparrow, the*
*frantic bellowing of the white tail deer.*

*The creation of a sad song, music of*
*the disinherited, abused by the*
*earth caretakers, what an ending to*
*what should have been a perfect melody.*

*Forest inhabitants in search*
*of a new home brought about*
*by man's search for more space,*
*destroying that which sustains us.*

*Where wisdom is assumed,*
*ignorance is not far behind.*

# The River's Edge

She ran vicariously every
day to the river's edge.
My bones would chill
of harm I dread.

For near she sought
to see beneath the waters,
a shadowy vision of a
figure with a ghostly laughter.

This is the game she played
at the river's edge,
with her unseen friends,
Lily and Fred.

Today, she brought to the
table, broken toys
and a golden frame
of a girl and boy.

To her mother and father she
spoke, this Lily and Fred.
They have a beautiful home
at the river's edge.

# To My Wilfe Elvira
# On Mother's Day

*Loving you these thirty-two years,*
*has instilled in me a great sense of*
*pride and urgency.*

*I can't wait to get home to tell*
*you about my day. You listen with*
*such intensity.*

*I feel as though nothing else matters*
*in my life at that moment as I*
*bare my soul to you.*

*I watch with intensity as your eyes light*
*up with joy and unbridled happiness*
*when you hear good news.*

*When my spirit is low, you immediately*
*sense the need to console me and take*
*me to a quiet place.*

*Your sense of dedication to family*
*is manifested in everything you do.*
*I truly adore you.*

*It is manifested in the love you show*
*when you are preparing food*
*or chastising our son.*

*It is manifested in the love you have*
*for all of your family and friends*
*and those who are less fortunate.*

*Above all, it is manifested in*
*your Christian faith that provides the*
*strength that guides and protects you.*

# Unlocking Mysteries

*In your presence, my masculinity*
*skips a time zone and*
*reverts back to childhood.*

*I find it almost impossible to*
*contain my passion*
*that aches to make itself known.*

*My historical self lies*
*dormant, but I eagerly wish*
*at times for its presence.*

*This is mystery of self denial,*
*trapped inside of me, these*
*explosive feelings in constant motion.*

*I have searched the deepest*
*depositories of my mind for an*
*answer to unlocking this mystery.*

*I long for a time that I can spend with you,*
*caressing your hair, your head*
*lying softly on my shoulder.*

*Touching you softly, gently caressing*
*your face. I can at times sense*
*your need for exploring the unknown.*

*I long to release this passion, destroy*
*this demon inside of me. To achieve*
*this, I must first unlock this mystery.*

# Visions

There are visions of illusions,
visions of grandeur,
inner visions from a dark place,
visions from the soul which
are visions of wisdom.

With visions of illusions,
we sometimes see that which is not,
with visions of grandeur,
we sometime seek unattainable goals.

Inner visions from a dark place,
causes us to battle with our own
demons. Visions from the soul can
lead us into the light of understanding.

It should first be understood that
all visions are portals that allows
good and evil to travel with equal
access on our road of discovery.

A clear state of mind and the
vision of wisdom are required if we are
to seek clarity and exactness of purpose
in and for our lives.

# The Journey

A great distance we have traveled
on land and sea,
with tidal waves and winds
of rage, placing
our lives in jeopardy.

This hazardous journey
and leap of faith,
has brought us to this land,
where the sun shines bright and
the days are filled with grace.

We give thanks to he who guided us
with keen eyes and mighty hands.
He carried us thru the tidal waves
to such a place of beauty
amidst the perils of the raging wind.

# The Smell Of Your Perfume

*The smell of your perfume*
*preceded you, the*
*darkness hid your image,*
*but could not hide your presence.*

*I, the hunter, pursued you*
*with and indescribable intensity,*
*determined to find you,*
*even in the darkness.*

*I heard footsteps, the sound was*
*faint, but with the wind*
*came that captivating aroma, I*
*knew I was close to you.*

*That piercing sound of stiletto*
*heels, was now pulsating*
*in my ears, the sweet smell*
*became even more defined.*

*From the moon lit street, I*
*can now see a shapely figure*
*moving suggestively; as if to*
*music meant for her ears only.*

*It became clear to me that*
*I was walking down my own street,*
*and the figure in the shadows was*
*standing in my doorway.*

# May I Speak Without Words

The blossom of my tree unwinds
to the mercy of your love.

May I speak without words?

For my love is not only blind
but also deaf.
The array of trenches that trapped
me is my teacher.

It instructs me to let go and explore,
never more imprisoned by my
unbalanced emotions, instead I have
instilled freedom within myself.

I have this key to a different strength,
the strength of another.

May I speak without words?

Another whose words touch me
to the point of ecstasy,
whose love lies hidden in the jungle
of letters and jumbled scripts.

May I speak without words?

Whose unspoken words are captured
in the form of a poem, meant to express
to portray my innermost feelings.

May I speak without words?

# The Willow Tree

The Willow tree with it's drooping
eyes filled with tears,
for centuries enslaved by the
Master's will.

For tall it stood in a stately fashion,
a giant shadow it cast,
with its magnificent foliage, covering
those who walked down its path.

Under it's protective canopy
were colorful umbrellas,
lavish dresses and songs sung
by slaves, I am my master's fellow.

In the nearby fields, there were no Willow
trees.  The scorching sun burned their skin.
There were no route of escape for
those slaves who wanted to leave.

Now, the master is gone, the slaves were set free.
The roads to freedom were filled with joy
and the sun was blocked by Willow trees.

# To My Wife, Elvira On
## MOTHER'S DAY

*Mother's Day has always
been my favorite day of the year.
I get the opportunity once again to give
praise to that which I hold so dear.*

*I am thankful that God saw in his
infinite wisdom to bring us together.
You have been patient through the
good times and stormy weather.*

*Through your eyes, I came to see
the true meaning of friendship and love,
because of the goodness of your heart,
I was transformed into a Dove.*

*Even though Mother's Day comes once a
year by a calendar that is man made.
I know that you are a mother all year long,
and that is why I give you praise*

*Forever Loving You
Your Loving Husband*

***Gamaliel***

### To My Wife, Elvira
### My Special Valentine

*This is the time of the year*
*we celebrate with words of love,*
*gifts of assorted candies, fine*
*linen, sparkling jewelry, trips*
*to romantic places and fine dining*

*All of this for the one we love.*

*But what is most impressive,*
*are those who have done all*
*the above all year long.*

*It should be remembered*
*that the value of a gift or gifts*
*are not measured by*

*cost of purchase, but the*
*love in which they were given.*

*Because you are my special*
*Valentine each and every*
*day of my life,*

*My special gift to you is my*
*everlasting commitment to*
*always love and cherish you.*

*And I will still give you gifts*

*Your loving husband*


*Gamaliel*

# *Happy Birthday*

*This time of year, our expectations are high,*
*especially when we are young.*
*Family, friends and that special someone,*
*sharing in our special day of fun.*

*We expect all sorts of things from*
*those who share our lives and space.*
*We sometime find ourselves reminiscing about*
*past birthdays in a quiet and isolated place.*

*It is always good to remember and reflect*
*on happy times and not the things we dread.*
*You see the quilt of happiness and sadness*
*are woven with the same thread.*

*So don't be misled by the melodious tones*
*and happiness portrayed as joy.*
*Beware of fleeting remnants of birthdays gone by*
*and little boys dreams and big boys toys.*

*Always remember that the true*
*meaning of a birthday is the gift of birth.*
*Experience it, share it and protect it*
*while you are on this earth.*

# Stranger In The Night

Tall and slender with
a body of perfect numbers.
Raven colored hair, sensuous
eyes that seem to penetrate as she
stares with such intensity.

I hesitate to engage in
a conversation for
fear of rejection.

Who am I to pursue this
beauty that seem to appear
from the shadows as a stranger
in the night.

As I turned away, I heard
foot steps, as I turned to look,
I could feel the heat of her
body, I could see the quivering

of her lips and heaving of
her breast as she stood
motionless.

And then she said, I am Brighten,
I am here for you.

# Taxing The Mind

*How far is the distance*
*between ignorance and awareness?*

*The time that is required to acquire knowledge.*

*How much time is required to acquire*
*knowledge?*

*That depends how diligent one is*
*in their pursuits.*

*What determines one's pursuits?*
*One's dreams and aspirations.*

*How does one realize their dreams?*

*Completing an acquired skill level*
*in their desired field of interest.*

# A True Friend

*How often we forget,*
*from whence we come,*
*with all our earthly trappings.*

*When our house was filled*
*with worldly goods and*
*bundles of Christmas wrapping.*

*The dark days came and*
*the thunder roared, and*
*the goods we had no more.*

*Of those who came and*
*shared our home,*
*no longer knocks at our door.*

*When all was well and*
*the future bright and of plenty,*
*there was no end.*

*The one I seldom saw at my table,*
*or making constant demands,*
*I discovered was my friend.*

*I am blessed to have you*
*as a true friend.*

# I Believe

*In him that created me
and gave me free will.
Instilled in me a sense of pride,*

*Blessed me with a healthy body
and sound mind.  Created
in me a sense of purpose.*

*Imprinted in my heart a true
road map to peace and happiness.
I am grateful for the use of*

*all of my limbs that allows me
take long walks thru
the fertile fields.*

*I am grateful for my sense of
hearing, that I may enjoy the songs
of the Mocking bird.*

*I am grateful for the feeling I get
when I touch the roses in my
mother's garden.*

*For all of these things, I am
truly grateful.*

# The Beauty of Nature

God created from his infinite source
these leaves from an Oak Tree.

With its many hues and
perfect symmetry.

We so quickly take for granted
our life source.

Why not do one good deed
each day on our daily course.

Reach out for an elderly hand,
A kind word to the disenfranchised.

Lift up the spirit of those who
might have been left by the wayside.

Be like the gentle Oak by the waters edge,
with its leaves of perfect symmetry.

It shares its foliage and tower of strength,
yet it serves as a shade tree.

# The Art of Learning

*For our destiny is not always
kind to us, sometimes it points
in the direction of a
path traveled less.*

*Our inspirational journey
with its flickering flames
shines bright in our darkest hours,
teaching us, preparing us for the text.*

*The books of learning, scholars
with their unsavory attitudes,
musty odors of historical buildings
reflects their process of learning.*

*But it is our diligence applied to study,
ultimately leads to the fulfillment of
accomplishing goals.  Our mind
becomes more discerning.*

# One Step

*In the dark we walk*
*with that dreadful fear of sinking.*
*in silence we stand*
*with that dreadful fear of thinking.*

*In life we think of death,*
*in doing so we are deceived.*
*What heights of glory are in our sights,*
*what wonders we could achieve*

*If only we could begin the journey*
*with one step of confidence.*
*Enjoying the experience given*
*with our creator's consent.*

# Christmas Without You

*How often I wondered what it would have*
*been like sitting in front of the fire place,*
*sipping champagne*
*and eating caviar.*

*Holding hands, looking into each others eyes,*
*admiring the beautifully decorated tree.*
*Listening to Christmas carols*
*by our favorite star.*

*The sharing of pass and present experiences*
*that completely engulfed our minds and spirit.*
*Sharing the good, bad and sad times,*
*the thought of gracefully growing old.*

*The passion that we fought so hard to hide,*
*camouflaged by a true friendship.*
*A friendship that grew gracefully over the*
*years, with and obvious need to bare our souls.*

*Instead, I am left with the*
*inevitable.*

*Christmas without you.*

# I wait

I find you inwardly beautiful,
outwardly fascinating,
easily accessible.

Soft to the touch,
strong of will,
in control of one's emotions.

Sculptured body,
englighten mind,
dept of soul.

Attacks reality,
follower of dreams,
still in touch with oneself.

Listens with a true heart,
speak from a place of visions, you
are unlike anyone I have ever known.

You seek not things that glitter
or made of silver or gold.
Listen, as I wait in the rain

I can hear your footsteps,
in the wind I hear your voice.
I wait patiently for the rain and

wind to cease, that I might
see your face and sit in a quiet
place and talk with you once again.

# My Brothers

*Unchained ankles,*
*unchallenged minds,*
*opportunity beckons.*
*The fields of degradation,*
*replaced by future anticipation.*
*For the void is no longer*
*shapeless or deep,*
*that, which once restricted,*
*no longer binds.*

*For the shape of our future*
*is woven by the golden threads of*
*wisdom that have always been*
*a part of our being.*
*Created by that which created all*
*things. Atom for atom, for*
*we are truly a part of the universe.*

*All that supports us and sustains*
*us, has been provided by he who is*
*omnipotent and omnipresent.*
*Hold our heads high, for we are*
*from a great source, a great*
*people, a great past, and*
*we have a great future.*

*And always remember*
*we are brothers*

# In Search of

Walking in a foreign land
looking for a friend.
Skin parched from the
hot desert sun.
Feet blistered from the
scorching desert sand.

In the distance I saw
a caravan of
camels as far as the
Eye could see.
In silence, he stretched
out his hand to me.

For I have met a merchant
in a foreign land, who would like
to be a friend, and asked
if I would join his caravan.

I am looking forward to
this journey that will take
me to strange lands.

# Poetic Quotations

*Picking up the pieces*
*of my past I left behind*
*from troubled times*

*Clarity of purpose*
*from experiences past of*
*lessons learned that last.*

*Justice seekers of history,*
*courts that reign supreme*
*working toward their schemes.*

*If I walk with you*
*in the troubled times,*
*will you be there in mine?*

*The calm wind from the*
*north that crystallizes spring,*
*that bring the flowers I idolize.*

*The long stem rose that is a*
*symbol of perfect symmetry,*
*embodies the uniqueness*
*of you and me.*

# The Beauty of A Black Woman

*The beauty of a black woman*
*transcends the spoken word.*
*The uprightness of her stature,*
*and the softness of her curves.*

*The strength of her convictions are*
*the under pending of her man.*
*She gives her love and devotion*
*with an attitude that says she can.*

*She can work an eight-hour job, come*
*home and prepare a gourmet meal.*
*Attend to the needs of the love of her life,*
*set back and enjoy the thrills*

*She can still look picture perfect*
*with nothing out of place.*
*After doing all of the above, she*
*is still the personification grace.*

# I Am Grateful

*In he that created me*
*and gave me free will.*
*Instilled in me a sense of pride.*
*Blessed me with a healthy*
*body and sound mind.*

*Created in me a sense of purpose.*
*Imprinted in my heart a true*
*road map to peace*
*and happiness.*

*I am grateful for my ability*
*to smell the perfumed flowers*
*that nature created and*
*painted so perfectly.*

*I am grateful for the use*
*of all of my limbs that allows*
*me to take long walks*
*thru the fertile land.*

*I am grateful for my sense*
*of hearing, that I may enjoy*
*the songs of the Mocking bird.*

*I am grateful for my sense of*
*feeling and smell when I touch*
*the roses in my mother's garden.*

*For all of these things, I am*
*truly grateful.*

# To Grandmother

*So many times Grandmothers are*
*over looked because we sometimes*
*forget that before they were*
*grandmothers, they were mothers.*

*How often we forget that it is*
*the patience and love of a mother*
*that instills in her children the*
*qualities of love, sharing, perseverance*
*and hope.*

*Because of these qualities,*
*her children will bring forth children,*
*and they will pass down the legacy of*
*their Grandmother's wisdom.*

*Now that you are a Grandmother,*
*you get to see the fruit of your labor.*

*We are truly blessed to have a Grandmother*
*that nurtured and guided our mothers.*

*Today we honor you Grandmother,*
*for the unselfish love and devotion*
*that you have given us all of our lives.*

*May God keep and bless you*
*We love you*
*Your Grand Children*

### *To My Wife Elvira*
### *God Created You for Me*

*I am truly thankful
for God giving me you.
Of all the things that I have
asked for, only God knew*

*The years ahead, the future
I could not see.
He who created my path,
prepared it for me.*

*Knowing that I am only as
strong as my weakest length.
God prepared for me
a pillar of strength.*

*For you have proven time and time
again, for me you were ordain.
For we don't know the ways of God,
but the end is always the same.*

*God paints a perfect picture,
and provides a perfect picture frame.*

# The Dangerous Pitfalls of Talking

*I have learned to listen to myself*
*for what it is worth,*
*with a deftly concern for word*
*definititons.*

*To listen cautiously, as I engage*
*in a conversation that uses*
*metaphors to explain truth, and how*
*different it is from fiction.*

*One must have an eagle's eye*
*and an uncanny sense of hearing,*
*to seek out those who would*
*use words to mislead.*

*It is with trickery, that the*
*treacherous use to engage those*
*who are eager to learn, and*
*those so easily deceived.*

*It is important to learn the word from its*
*roots, before spreading your wings.*
*Remember, it is always good to*
*know the beginning of things.*

*An unskilled engagement in conversation*
*with a learned person,*
*will provide no avenue of escape,*
*and the charlatan will have no diversion.*

# The Teacher

The art of learning from anyone
could be described as your teacher.

As all voices heard could be
described as the speaker.

As the orgin of an ocean
could be traced to a stream.

As the completion of all great
projects can be traced to a dream.

For I have learned to be humble
in the face of impending danger.

My acquired wisdom has prevented
me from being snared by strangers.

And yet I struggle with myself as
I go about my daily life.

How much have I learned from
teachers's advice?

I have learned to humble
Myself to the wisdom of life

# *Energy*

*How much energy are you prepared*
*to spend running a negative mile?*

*How much energy are you prepared*
*to spend, turning a frown into a smile?*

*How much energy are you prepared*
*to spend creating negative space?*

*How much energy are you prepared*
*to spend in search of a quiet place.*

# My Great Discovery

*That which you have longed for,*
*You have finally found,*
*The golden fleece and David's crown.*

*What magical spells can you raise*
*from the historical graves,*
*for the dead don't always speak,*
*there is nothing they crave.*

*They have the best of both worlds,*
*they have lived the earthly side,*
*some in beauty and peace.*

*From beneath the earth in their timeless*
*tombs in which they now reside.*
*Thy watch what you are doing with*
*David's crown and The golden fleece.*

*Who would dare wear David's crown,*
*a heavenly wisdom they must have,*
*maybe a worthy one has been found.*
*Only then would he share.*

*Maybe those of whom we speak, they*
*too, would be worthy of David's crown*
*And the golden fleece.*

# There Are No Boundaries
## To The Soul

*Cities of old, our mind does visit with*
*Some degree of accuracy, from dreams*
*On wings of gold.*

*Night flight, guided by the moon and*
*Stars, unimpeded by earthly obstacles.  There*
*Are no boundaries to the soul.*

*Fear not to dream of distant places where*
*The waters are icy blue and the flowers*
*Smiles in your face.*

*Flap your wings of gold.  You will find*
*Yourself on a moon-lit island, with*
*Your soul in a quiet place.*

*Your mind will be free to roam*
*The heavens, and talk with the*
*Angels of old.*

*Once again, you will witness that there*
*Are no boundaries to the soul.*

*You will dream of the creator's wisdom*
*Who existed before the earth was formed.*

*Your head shall rest upon his bosom*
*And all of your worries will be gone.*

# The Coliseum Of Rome

*To travel these lands in different parts of the world*
*is a wonderful experience, it soothes the soul,*
*purifies the heart and enlightens one's mind.*

*Ignorance is the conduit for prejudices of*
*race, ideas, commitment and growth.  And*
*yet we strive to attain the greatest measure*
*of wisdom, that is love for one another.*

*Elasticing one's mind, whether through*
*the media, classroom, travel or normal*
*conversation, will serve you well as*
*you go about your daily life.*

*What a beautiful place, historical Rome*
*must have been with its majestic*
*buildings and creative art forms.*

*The greatest minds of the ages once walked*
*the great halls, class rooms, and streets, read in*
*the great libraries, taught in the great schools.*

*And the wicked in the end, brought about*
*the destruction.  Just think about the*
*irony of it all.*

# Here I Stand

*I am waiting patiently*
*for the right person*
*to come into my life.*

*Where is she, I asked*
*myself constantly. I can*
*think of nothing else.*

*Life stands still for me now.*
*I am stuck in what seem*
*to be an eternity.*

*I will think of something*
*funny. But I must not*
*displace this serious thought*
*with folly.*

*I will just stand.*

*Here I Stand.*

# In Memory Of My Brother Donald

*"Natures Harmony"*

*In the spring when the flowers*
*comes out of their closet and adorn*
*their robes of many colors.*
*Nature's harmony is on display.*

*In the fall when the trees changes*
*their cloak to an array of glorious*
*colors and the sweet aroma fill the air.*

*When the winter icicles hangs from*
*tree limbs and crystal white snow*
*covers the land and the snow birds visits.*
*Nature's harmony is on display.*

*In the summer when the beaches*
*are filled with family and friends,*
*and laughter fills the air and when*
*people are rushing to get home.*

*When all seasons have passed*
*and life has been a joy, I can look*
*back on all of the seasons, and say, I*
*have had a full life, I was loved by all*
*My family and friends.*

*I have finally reached my heavenly*
*destination and I am at peace.*

*Nature's harmony is till on display.*

# God's Glory

*I have watch with great anticipation*
*the miracles in my life.*

*The indelible foot prints*
*of his mercy.*

*I am reminded by my existence,*
*the many pitfalls I have avoided, because*
*I have allowed him to guide me.*

*I am grateful to have his words to*
*stand on and his promise of*
*restoration.*

*All that was taken from me,*
*has been replaced ten fold.*

*For there are many mansions in my father's*
*house.  His store houses are over flowing*

*His mercy endures forever*

# A Dedication
# To Mother

*A gentle giant and matriarch of a*
*family deeply rooted in religious values*
*and principles.  Based on the concept,*
*if the will is there, so is the way.*

*A nurturing mother to eleven children,*
*never tiring from dusts to dawn.  Blessed*
*with a fixed mind and a pure heart.  A*
*termination to survive all of the ordeals*
*that life would present.*

*She always returned to her basic concept,*
*if the will is there, so is the way.*
*She in her twilight years, her determination*
*has not waned.*

*She is even more determine today,*
*to instill in her children, the core values*
*of love of God, love of self, and love*
*for one another.  This is the glue that binds.*

*Our mother is the force behind who we are*
*and what we have become.  She has given*
*us a road map to love and happiness and*
*spiritual success.*

*Spiritual success opens the doors to*
*earthly success, if we would only love*
*and respect one another.*

*Thank you mother, for being a real mother.*
*Thank you for always being there for*
*all of us.*

# A Perfect Blend

*Your eyes are like the clear blue*
*waters of the Caribbean Islands,*
*skin the color of their beaches, like*
*golden sand.*

*Delicate as the flowers that beautifies,*
*mystify and blends so perfectly*
*with the land.*

*A voice that is soft and rhythmic,*
*melodic at every pitch.*
*The smell of your perfume ignites*
*the fire within me.*

*The shadows of passion intrudes*
*in my dreams, does battle with my soul,*
*and never will I defeat thee.*

# I Am Just A Bee

*Flying around all day*
*viewing the world from*
*a bee's perspective.*

*I see the smiles and tears.*

*Tears of the children*
*in South East Washington, D.C.*
*the suffering of children*
*in Ethiopia.*

*I see smiles of the privilege*
*in Georgetown, Saudi Arabia,*
*playing in the front yards*
*of their palatial homes.*

*I see the hatred that emanates*
*from misunderstanding*
*our neighbors.*

*I witnessed first hand the*
*abuse and slaughter of the*
*disenfranchised.*

*And yet, our civilized world*
*stands by with all of their*
*technology and resources and*
*watches with great anticipation,*
*as the slaughter continues.*

*I see the smiles and tears,*
*but who am I*

*I Am Just A BEE*

# Poison

*Dreary days and*
*endless nights, tormented*
*by man made dreams*
*and endless schemes.*

*Smoky clubs on*
*Sunset Boulevard, needle*
*infested alleyways,*
*and little girls that pimps craves.*

*I long to rid myself of this self*
*imposed prison of degradation*
*of suffering and endless pain.*
*If there is no suffering, there is no gain.*

*I have discovered that my*
*many friends are few.*
*The many used me to no end.*
*The few helped me to begin again.*

# The Good I Have Done

*I have always thought of*
*good deeds to do,*
*in those who good deeds are few.*

*To toss a slice of bread and a*
*piece of meat to*
*those who have none.*

*Thoughts of kindness I have and*
*good deeds I have done.*

*When the lights are dim and*
*the road nears it's in.*

*I will have no regrets, I will just*
*begin again.*

# The Inevitable

*Allow yourself to dream
the most perfect dream, while
acknowledging that it is
a dream of imperfection.*

*It is with that acknowledgement,
that you have come face to face
with your true self, and fear
or reality will dissipate.*

*At that point in your life,
the inevitable is realized as
an integral part of your being.*

*You will have discovered that
an attempt to block the
inevitable is impossible.*

# Pit Falls Of The Heart

How often we allow what don't belong,
the opportunity of introduction.

We a trusting people by nature, believe
the good is inherent in all of us.

We fail to remember that there is
a duality that dwells in us, good and evil.

Only those who fully understand that
evil is real in the world, will have

the opportunity of aligning themselves
with the good of this world.

One's thought process is the beginning
stage that will provide a viable

solution for waging a war that begins
in the heart of all us.

So let us begin with the clarity of purpose,
which is to sustain the good in us, which
is our true purpose for existing.

# Crystal

*Crystal is the personification*
*of purity, strength and light.*
*It has a multifaceted of infusions*
*that exemplifies your life in*
*different stages.*

*It is flawless in its mirrored image,*
*which exemplifies the perfection*
*of God's creation and his infinite wisdom*
*involved in his thought process.*

*The strength of crystal is a*
*relflection of the binding process*
*of you, that gives you the will to excel,*
*even in times of trials and tribulations.*

*The unique artistry involved in the*
*creation of crystal is a reflection of*
*your inner and outer beauty, which is*
*reflected in everything you do.*

*The fire that emanates from crystal*
*reflects your zest for life and*
*your unyielding desire to reach*
*out to others.*

*It is this zest for life that*
*enables you to survive where*
*others would fail.*

# Stripping the Soul

*In the beginning, history speaks of*
*a historical people, which was promised*
*a perfect future to be lived in a perfect*
*land filled with milk and honey.*

*This expectation of the creator was*
*short lived. It was because of free will,*
*that the human race was unable to*
*maintain the alignment with the creator*
*that was intended.*

*Because of mans inability to accept*
*the fact that to succeed is based on*
*his obedience, will continue to*
*cause catastrophic changes*
*in their lives.*

*They will continue to strip their*
*Souls of the laws that were*
*implanted in the beginning, that*
*was to be humanities road map*
*to the life that was promised.*

*The good new is, the ending*
*has already been written and the*
*creator's intended purpose for*
*man will be realized.*

# Nature's Game Plan

*Nature has a way of reminding*
*us who is in charge.*

*When we think we are in control of*
*our lives, the inevitable*
*shows its face.*

*Confronted with the dark side,*
*we seek a safe place.*

*Only to be reminded that we*
*have no place to hide*

*From nature's barrage*
*of trials by faith.*

# Lend Me Your Ears

I am always talking to the wall,
My voice appears to vibrate in the wind.
When asked to explain what I said,
I have to start all over again.

Lend me your ears that
I may share with you my thoughts.
I am eager to impart with you
Something other then what I brought.

The material things you seem to enjoy,
Silver and gold and flora ensemble.
I seek only to enjoy your company
And for that I am truly humble.

Lend me your ears that I might
Share with you my childhood dreams.
All the things I longed for but could not own.
I have learned the true value of simple things.

Have learned that to listen is to learn,
I have given thought to those without ears.
Value in words to those who listen is a gem.
I have been far from the truth, and yet so near.

I finally discovered the secret to life's success.
The inner voice of the soul is in control,
I now listen with serious intentions.
I now marvel at the stories untold.

# The Walk

*I have always walked with great*
*Intention and clarity of purpose,*
*Even though I was truly blind.*

*One must not refuse to look at*
*One if one hopes to seek*
*justice and truth.*

*The reality of being must always*
*Begin with the center. From*
*The center the energy flows*
*That lends fire to all truth.*

*This energy allows one to pursue*
*With diligence, vigor and some*
*Degree of clarity of one's true*
*Purpose for existing.*

*At the end of your journey,*
*You will have understood the*
*True meaning of the walk*

# A Field Of Music

*When I was young I would*
*spend large amounts of time*
*walking between the corn*
*rows listening to the wind as*
*it made those melodic sounds.*

*When I became an adult, I*
*remembered those sounds. I*
*discovered that it contained the*
*violin, piano and the heavenly*
*harp that produced soft melodies.*

*I don't recall loud horns or*
*big drums. I remembered that the*
*music flowed evenly. I*
*recalled asking myself how*
*was this possible.*

*From above the clouds a voice*
*shouted! Your mind was in tune*
*to musical instruments of nature.*
*A symphony, I had created*
*just for you.*

*As a child your mind was*
*clear and pure which allowed*
*me to commune with you*
*through a field of music.*

*It is good that your spirit*
*has remembered me. I continue*
*to walk with you down the*
*corn rows of life.*

# Life's A Flower Bed

The flower bed of life are
a mix of very delicate flowers,
their petals are easily blown away
with the slightest wind shift.

Like life, flowers are not always
rooted in fertile ground and they are
not always deeply rooted. In some
cases, their roots are shallow and
delicately planted in unproductive soil.

Like life, one of the most beautiful
of all flowers, the rose, are attached
to long stems, with penetrating
thorns that will inflict pain.

I would suggest that like a flower
bed, careful planning of life soil
should be properly treated, the thought
process should be properly seeded.

Our direction should be properly
motivated and our intentions
should be deeply rooted, to
ensure that we are not deterred
from our journey.

We are ultimately responsible
for our own flower bed. Whether
it becomes a bed of roses with
painful thorns, or a beauty that
enhances our lives is the question.

Have we become mature and
advanced enough to deal

with the pain of growth from
the penetrating thorns of life.

# Take My Hand

*Here we are my dear,*
*standing before the judgement*
*of God and man.*

*Acknowledging my love for you,*
*when the winter storms come*
*just take my hand.*

*I promise to wipe away all of your*
*tears caused by the unforeseen,*
*as we journey across this land.*

*Without fear, we will face life, and*
*go where no one has gone before.*
*Just take my hand.*

# The Reality of Failure

*When we open the door of accepting
without exception, we are limited in
our ability to retreat without the
possibility of causing pain to those
we hold most dear.*

*To give of ourselves without thought
of some degree of latitude, in
some ways speaks to the legitimacy,
that all men are fools when it
comes to the desires of the heart.*

*We thrive on success, failing to realize
that success was first discovered
by the reality of failure.  Failure
should be treated as a gem of great
value.  It builds character.*

*Failures lessen the growing pains
from birth to human reality,
from childhood to adulthood, and
ultimately to the true realization
of being.*

*In the end, the reality of failure is
the tangible product that allows
us to see the results of greatness in
human development and
achievement.*

# Leverage

*I have set down with myself*
*took out all of my measuring tools*
*to ensure that all my dreams*
*will come to fruition.*

*I have looked for leverage in what appears*
*to be all of the right places.*

*I have held conferences with*
*influential friends, attended*
*accredited schools of learning.*

*I have put into practice what I have*
*learned. In return, I have received great wealth,*
*made great friends, but an emptiness remains.*

*I repeated my journey seeking*
*leverage. I discovered the main*
*ingredient that was missing.*

*I had not searched my soul*
*that is where the real leverage*
*for success rest.*

*I discovered that wealth does*
*not replace things of true substance.*
*I discovered that true friends*
*are earned through time and patience.*

*One must be able to bare one's soul,*
*discard all barriers that would prevent*
*a friend from sharing your space.*

*A true friend is eager to share your*
*happiness, your sadness, your*
*disappointment and your accomplishments.*

*So leverage comes in the discovery*
*of truth. The truth of self discovery.*

# Maintenance of Our
# Religious History

*It is often overlooked what it takes to
prepare for Sunday's services. The many
hours the Pastors spends in preparation
for the right words for their congregation.*

*It is often overlooked, the many hours
that the choir spends diligently practicing
the right hymns that will uplift and inspire.*

*So many times the congregation is so rapped
up in their enjoyment, that they forget
the dedicated Christians that make it all
possible by and through the will of God.*

*Sometimes we take for granted the valued
contribution of the church. The dedicated
elders that embodies the religious faith
of the church.*

*The value contribution of the youth
that embodies the future of the church.
The valued contribution of those
dedicated volunteers who give unselfishly
of their time assisting in the upkeep
and prosperity of the church.*

*Lets not forget those dedicated Christians
who volunteer their time in our community,
visiting the sick and shut in. Those who
carry the biblical teachings to the
disenfranchised.*

*Let us not forget the members of the church,
that through their contributions, sustains the
church, which enables the church
to do God's will.*

# To My Wife Elvira On Her Sixtieth Birthday

*Sixty years is cause to sing in
celebration of a gentle life.*

*Happy Birthday to the Mother
And the wife.*

*Taking pleasure in what
Love might bring.*

*Yearning for what's worth
the treasuring.*

*Your birthday is very special to me
because I have you in my life.*

*It is even more special to me,
because you are my wife.*

*Your loving husband*

*Gamaliel*

# This Light

*We need this light that once again shines among us. This light that brings hope, the realization of dreams past.*

*This light that will point the way to a rediscovery of a world filled with love, peace and hope for all people.*

*This light that will remove the obstacles that plagues this nation that has been so deeply rooted in our souls.*

*We must look at the state of this world as it really is, and have the vision to create a path that will reestablish this world as it was intended to be.*

*It is in this man that I believe embodies the spirit that will allow this country to bring one family to the table of negotiation.*

*I believe this man is not only a visionary with a dream, but the key to the gateway of this dream.*

*Let's not allow our insecurities and our hidden prejudices prevent us as a people from picking up the banner of peace and prosperity that have been once again handed to us.*

*Let all of us ride the coattails of this man dreams, Barack Obama.*

# Barack Obama

*He has been elected by a higher*
*source to travel this road less traveled,*
*with a true willingness to confront*
*the demons of centuries pass.*

*He has picked up the banner of*
*those who have given their lives*
*that he might have this great*
*opportunity to share his dreams*
*without regard for color or class.*

*He brings to the world a vision*
*of unity equality, a united*
*America, that will serve as a beacon*
*for all those that seek access*
*to these shores.*

*He dreams of a world that provides*
*safety without the threat of war, where*
*there are  no longer the disenfranchised,*
*where no one will be denied basic needs*
*of life, where there are no closed doors.*

# Country Air

*Living where traffic is slow,*
*noise reduced to silence.*
*Living where one of my most favorite*
*places to go is the Country Fair.*

*Looking forward to the long*
*freight train that breaks the*
*monotony of the silent days,*
*looking to inhale the country air.*

*Spending most of my day admiring*
*the green fields of beans and corn,*
*the oversized machinery that*
*march up and down like the overseer.*

*The sprinklers that encompasses*
*a hundred rows, and rolls along like*
*it has a mind of its own.  Like the marching*
*machine, it changes it own gears.*

*I have come to enjoy the quietness*
*of days, and the stillness of the nights.*
*The smell of fresh peas and corn*
*produced by fertile fields.*

*I have come to admire the rolling giants*
*that till the soil, water the rows that*
*seem endless.  I find myself waiting*
*patiently for the farmers yield.*

*I have noticed that my breathing*
*is without effort, less stress from city life.*
*For what reasons the change I don't care.*
*I give all the credit to the country air*

# The Miracle Flower

Each morning I watched from
my window hoping to see
this fragile flower
spring to life.

With intensity, I watched as
the sun set.  I wish
for a light shower to dampen
its petals and energize its roots.

The coolness of morning comes,
light sprinkles from a warm rain
beats gently on its petals
and trickles down its stems.

I watch with a child's curiosity
as the stems dark green color
returns, and the drooping petals
once again displays its vigor.

Once again we are reminded of
the beauty of nature, and its
power of restoration.

# Bearing The Cross

*We sometimes take for granted for*
*that which has been given freely. It required*
*no effort on our part. And because*
*of that, some of us show no*
*gratitude or appreciation.*

*This generation bears the cross of change*
*we hope for. But I still wonder how*
*far will man go to maintain the*
*monopoly on self gratification.*

*Man continues to refuse to bear*
*the cross that was left behind*
*by those who gave freely of their blood.*

*We who refuse to pray to Yahweh, the*
*creator of the heavens and earth, he*
*who gives freely of his love.*

*What have one achieved during*
*their quest for fortune and fame, other*
*then worn out shoes, and musty clothes.*

*We who have chosen to ignore*
*his name, and the miracle flight*
*of the searching dove.*

# The Miracle of Christmas

*I remember having little as a child,*
*perhaps a broken bicycle,*
*or a crippled toy.*

*I remember having old clothes*
*cleaned and pressed, with a mother's*
*love and Christmas joy.*

*I remember sitting at the table*
*On Christmas morning with a little*
*Bread and a little meat.*

*I remember my father and my mother*
*saying, be grateful for what God has*
*provided for us to eat.*

*I remember my mother saying, be*
*thankful for the miracle of Christmas,*
*and the most important sacrifice.*

*Be thankful for God's decision*
*to give his son, Jesus Christ, who*
*paid the ultimate price.*

*It is because of my parents teaching*
*me to appreciate small things. I was able*
*to receive the repairing of my heart.*

*I will forever be grateful for your*
*skill, compassion and care. And don't*
*forget that God set the stage, and played*
*the ultimate part.*

# I Am Not Alone

Using the night to hide myself,
from those who seek my life.
Using the day to show myself,
to those that will join my fight.

Using the wisdom of time and place,
to do battle in the devil's domain.
using the book of the historical saints,
to this victory I will lay claim.

For in this battle, I am not alone,
my faith over powers my fears.
My weapons have been carefully honed,
all down thru the years.

# Remembering The Walk

*I remember the long walks thru*
*the wooded area behind my home.*

*The paths were covered with pine*
*straw, needles and cones.*

*I enjoyed the past experiences*
*that crowded my mind.*

*I found myself sharing them*
*with my favorite felines.*

*They always accompanied me*
*on my nature walks.*

*It was almost like they understood*
*my every thought.*

*The paths are now covered with vines.*
*the tall pines cut down by man.*

*Only the memory remains of my felines.*

# A Preacher's Life

One of choice would be easy to say.
That is not the case in most assignments.

True ministry requires God's intervention,
And must be blessed with God's consent.

Man's belief that fortune and fame,
Is acquired by the use of his own power.

Religious ministry works only in his name,
And not in the hands of cowards.

What man does not understand,
He has no power of his own.

Thru the ages he has tempted God's hand,
But God's plan cannot be undone.

The devil knows that hell is his home,
He seeks to corrupt as many souls as he can.

In the end the devil and the corrupt stands alone.
The God of the universe is still in command.

The Preacher's journey is a perilous one,
His life is not his own.

Delivering the message as it is written
Is his goal until God calls him home.

# The Death Of My Master

I remember walking among the trees
of my master, longing to forget the
heat of the day.

My hands were sore from holding
that old pitch falk that I used
for tossing the hay.

I remembered the master's
voice as he called from the main house.
Don't forget to bring wood for the stove.

Don't forget to check the clothes line, the
wife wants to make sure that you
bring in all the clothes.

That's my master, he treats me well.
Always make sure I get the leanest meat,
and a double helping of shortbread.

I still dream of the day that I'll
be free to find my way home.  A
loud voice came from the main house,
the master is dead.

I thought to myself, my prayers have
been answered, now the journey begins.
This journey of freedom that I hold so dear.

I discovered that the home I longed for
was on this land that I labored
all of these years.

The master's wife agreed, as she
wiped away her tears.

Printed in the United States
by Baker & Taylor Publisher Services